Scribner
1230 Avenue of the
Americas
New York, NY 10020

# WHO'S GOT GAME?

The Ant or the Grasshopper?

TONI & SLADE MORRISON
pictures by PASCAL LEMAITRE

SCRIBNER and design are trademarks of Macmillan Library Reference USA, Inc., used under license by Simon & Schuster, the publisher of this work.

DESIGNED by Pascal Lemaitre; colors by P. Lemaitre & E. Phuon.

Manufactured in the United States of America.
10 9 8 7 6 5 4 3 2 1

Library of Congress Cataloging-in-Publication Data
Morrison, Toni.
   The ant or the grasshopper? / by Toni Morrison
                                 and Slade Morrison;
        illustrated by Pascal Lemaitre.
   p. cm. - (Who's got game?)

   1. Aesop's fables—Adaptations. 2. Fables, American.
   I. Morrison, Slade. II. Lemaitre, Pascal. III. Title.

   PS3563.O8749 A58 2003
   741.5'973—dc21                      2002030486

      ISBN: 0-7432-2247-4

For INFORMATION regarding special discounts
for bulk purchases, please contact
Simon & Schuster Special Sales at
1-800-456-6798 or
business@simonandschuster.com

to my mother
P.L.

to Kali-Ma
and E.A.

T.M.+S.M.

One hot day as they lay in the shade Kid A turned to his friend and said:
Got to split, Foxy. The summer's been fun
Time to dump this place, get back in the race. There's a lot of work to be done.
Hold on, I just thought of a tune.
Listen up, kid. This will rocket the moon!

Foxy raised his wings, rubbed them hard, making music so def it drew a crowd.

That's cool, Foxy G, but listen to me.

Vacation is gone; the days getting short. We can't hang forever on the basketball court!

Then split, Kid A.

Who's in your way?

As for me, Foxy G...

I have to let my music out!

Hard at work or fast asleep,
he couldn't stop his dancing feet

He fixed the stove, raked the leaves,
covered the shrubs so they wouldn't freeze.

He heaped and piled and baked
and stored
jam to be spread
on slices of bread.

When winter howled at the door.

Still out in the park was Foxy G
where the wind began to bite.
He wanted to finish one more tune
before the coming night.
Unfolding his wings from a cardboard box

Battling shame he left the park.
There was nothing else to do
but swallow his pride and drag his wings
back to the neighborhood.
Trying not to shake, to break or quake,

He knocked on Kid A's door.

I'm cold kid, with nothing to eat.
My wings are freezing and I'm dead on my feet.
I'm not going to make it out here with no heat.
So, say, my friend. Can I come in?

Kid A munched a doughnut and scoped his friend.

He knew he was pitiful and ought to say "please."
But his pride returned as he fell to his knees.
I quenched your thirst and fed your soul, you can't spare me a doughnut hole?

Foxy stumbled off into the night his head held high, his arms wrapped tight around his wings with all his might.

His day is darkest when I leave
with all my music up my sleeve.
Name, fame, blame, shame -
The question is: who's got game?